FORGOTTEN TALES

Stories from the Kashmir Valley

Sana Altaf

Leadstart

INKSTATE

ISBN: 978-93-9004-098-8

© Sana Altaf, 2022

First published in India 2022 by Leadstart Inkstate
A brand of One Point Six Technologies Pvt. Ltd.

123, Building J2, Shram Seva Premises,
Wadala Truck Terminal,
Mumbai 400022, Maharashtra, INDIA
Phone: +91 96999 33000
Email: info@leadstartcorp.com
www.leadstartcorp.com

Disclaimer: This is a work of fiction. All the names, characters, businesses, places, events and incidents in this book are either the product of the author's imagination or used in a fictitious manner. Any resemblance to actual persons, living or dead, or actual events is purely coincidental.

Editor: Shayoni Mitra
Cover: Ami Parekh
Layouts: Kevis Tech

*Thank you, Mom and Dad, for
being there, always …*

Contents

About the Author

Sana Altaf was born in winter in Kashmir. As she learned to take her first steps and utter her first words, the world around her was changing. She was hardly five-year-old when she first heard the gunshots as she played slide on the snow. From that day, nothing remained the same. She grew up with blasts, killings, protests, and unending strikes.

As she began to gain an understanding of what was happening around her, her heart never felt at ease. She began expressing herself through writing and chose journalism as her career. She won an award in 2013 for reporting about women's issues during conflict.

Backed by 10 years of journalism experience, she is currently based in the United Arab Emirates where she pursues her passion for writing.

Forgotten Tales is her first collection of short stories.

1

Memory of the Father

A black and white picture hung from the wall of her room. It was the only memory Ayesha had of her father. The picture had become the face of her struggle from the age of five. It was the first time when she carried the framed picture all the way to Srinagar, sat with a group of women, and stared curiously at the media persons.

The practice became a ritual of her life which she silently followed for years. It was only when she grew up, that Ayesha, who was now eighteen, understood that her father had disappeared after being taken away by the security forces seventeen years back. She was hardly a year old then.

Her mother, Zaina, had taken up the task of tracing her husband tirelessly for years. But after she became bedridden, the picture only haunted Ayesha.

Every time she looked at it, she felt a pressing responsibility on her. She was overtaken by a strong sense of guilt. She felt she had done an injustice to her father, whom she hardly remembered, and more to her mother, who spent her entire youth trying to find her husband.

Ayesha could not take the burden to her grave. She could not let her mother die without declaring to her if she was a widow or a half widow.

She decided to start a fight of her own. To hunt for a man, whom she hardly remembered seeing. The picture—

where a man in his late 30's stood dressed in a blue-collared shirt against the poster of meadows pasted on the wall of a local photo studio, with a white cap on his head. His face clean-shaven, looked fairer while his brown eyes sparkled with the flash from the camera—this would be her only weapon.

But where would she find her father?

After striking a few conversations with her mother, who was now ageing fast, Ayesha learnt that her father was taken away by security forces from their home.

She remembered it was during the core winter of January when they were preparing to have dinner that they heard a knock at the door. The security forces barged into the house, taking Ayesha's father, suspecting him to be a sympathiser of militants. For days, weeks, and months, there was no news.

Zaina had lodged an FIR, the investigation for which was hardly done. She had met politicians, leaders, and activists who promised support; but her husband was never found.

That night, Ayesha charted out a mental plan. First, she would visit the concerned police station and follow up on the status of the seventeen-year-old FIR. She would personally follow the case with the police. She would pay bribes if needed, to get the truth out.

The next morning, without telling her mother the truth, Ayesha walked to the police station.

The police station was hardly a twenty-minute walk from her home. As she reached the large rusting iron gate of the police station, she stopped.

A strange sense of fear seized her. She had never been to a police station before. She didn't know what she would face. *It would either be victory or failure*, she said to herself.

It took her a few minutes to prepare herself for the questions she would have to answer at the station.

Suddenly, the picture hanging on her wall flashed before her eyes. Ayesha saw herself in the arms of the man in the picture. Her small body cuddled in the warmth of his arms. She stirred and stepped inside the gate. No sooner did she step in, when she was met with the mysterious gaze of the police officers scattered randomly around the compound of the station.

"Madam, where are you going?" one of them shouted.

"I need to see the station officer," she answered, walking briskly towards the SHO's room.

The officer's conversation on his phone seemed to be never-ending as she stood waiting at the door. Her eyes examined the dark room that smelt of tobacco. Piles of files randomly rested on his table. Finally, the officer finished with the call.

"So, what brings you here, madam?" said the stubborn-looking man.

"Theft or marital dispute?"

"I am looking for my father. He has been missing for seventeen years," she answered.

"I need a copy of the FIR that was filed years ago and want to know what happened to the case."

The officer told her that it was impossible to find the details of such an old case.

"Our building had caught on fire seven years back and all of the older records were lost. I have been here for just three years. I am afraid I can't be of any help."

Heartbroken, Ayesha left the police station.

Her mind wandered as she walked her way home. Her first hope was lost. But she would not give up.

Weeks ago, she recalled reading in a newspaper about a few human rights activists working to trace disappeared persons. She spent most of the night scanning through the newspapers. She jotted down their names and designations.

From what Ayesha read in the newspapers, they were all based in Srinagar. She decided to travel the next day and seek help from them.

It was past ten in the morning. She stood waiting outside the office of Niyaz, one of the prominent human rights activists. The newspaper clippings hanging from the wall caught her attention. Many focused on the plight of the families of disappeared persons. She was confident about finding some clues about her father.

Niyaz gave her a patient hearing and assured her of all the help possible. However, Ayesha was sad to know that amongst the thousands of persons who had disappeared, none had been traced so far.

"The cases are being fought at the human rights commission. You can file your case too and see if we can get somewhere."

By now Ayesha was sure that filing such a case would only mean years of attending court with no result.

A week passed. Ayesha spent most of her time taking care of her ailing mother.

The daily chores, cooking, and cleaning kept her busy, but her mind was static on her aim. There were times when she thought of giving it all up, but looking at her mother revived all her pain.

One afternoon while serving lunch to her mother, she asked her where all the disappeared persons went.

"We had heard that they are taken to camps or interrogation centres. That's all I know," said her mother.

Zaina had visited a few interrogation centres with the hope of finding her husband. Every time she tried, she was shoved away by the security personnel at the gate.

That night, lying silent in her bed, Ayesha imagined her father being interrogated, tortured, and lying lifeless in an imaginary interrogation centre.

What if he is still inside one of them, waiting for help from family? she thought to herself.

There was nothing more she thought of before deciding to visit the interrogation centres to find her father. She would cry and plead before the people there to help her figure out where her father was.

The next morning brought a new hope for Ayesha.

She knew a few interrogation centres in her town and in Srinagar from her monthly visits for sit-ins. She planned to visit the most notorious interrogation centre she knew in her town first. Those arrested from her village were lodged in that interrogation centre.

The local bus dropped her over half a kilometre from where the interrogation centre stood. Clad in a black abaya[1], she felt confident that no one would recognize her.

She walked with strong, hopeful steps; her mind full of confusing thoughts. Just as she neared the place, she felt confused and tense about how to approach the entire matter. She stood outside the mighty wired walls of the centre. The massive iron gates were guarded by tall bunkers. Security forces peered through the clumsy bunkers, with the nook of their guns pointed towards the road.

Ayesha slowly walked to the gate.

---

[1] Long, loose robe mostly worn by Muslim women

Suddenly, she shrank at a roaring voice asking her to stop. Three security personnel emerged from one of the bunkers and walked towards her.

"Why are you here," one of them asked.

"My father has gone missing. I want to know if he was lodged here."

"Why would he be here?"

"He was taken away by security forces and has not returned."

"When?" asked one of the security personnel.

"Seventeen years ago."

The whole group of security personnel guarding the entrance burst into laughter.

"So, you think he will be here for seventeen years, enjoying himself, waiting for you to come take him?"

Her face turned red as she remembered her mother. She felt rage run through her blood. She could not take the humiliation any further.

She picked up a huge piece of brick lying nearby and aimed it at one of the security personnel.

The man fell to the ground, blood oozing from his head. Her head was spinning with anger and she wanted to hit again. But soon, she was grabbed by what seemed like a whole contingent of policewomen.

There was an outcry all over the place. She did not realize how many times she was slapped, but she could hardly hear any of the voices that surrounded her. Two women personnel stifled her arms. She was taken to a dark room with a huge iron gate. Ayesha did not realize what was happening until she saw herself locked behind a giant door. There were no windows in the room. The place smelt of urine. She could see only her dark shadow on the wall.

Her eyes grew sore from the constant weeping. She didn't know if she was sorry for her decision. In her heart, she had some hope that she might find her father there. Maybe, he was lying in a similar room somewhere.

Her heart pained as she thought of her mother. She had not informed anyone about what she was doing, or where she was going. No one would know where she was! Her mother's face flashed before her eyes, bringing a strong sense of guilt.

She didn't know how long it had been when the door of her room opened.

"You girl, come out," said a female police officer standing at the door.

Ayesha's heart rejoiced at the thought of her release. As she stood up, the woman held her arm tightly, dragging her across the cold dark corridor.

"Where are you taking me?" Ayesha asked.

"You know what you have done. You can't go like this," the woman replied.

"I just want to find my father," she reiterated while being pushed inside a closed room.

Suddenly Ayesha felt a sting in her arm. Before she could comprehend what was happening, she collapsed on the ground. She lost consciousness as the door behind her slammed close.

A sudden knock at the door stirred Zaina from her sleep. Supporting herself with a staff, she hurriedly rushed to the door, sure that her daughter was back.

She opened the door, but Ayesha was not there. She called her name, repeatedly, to see if she was around, but it was all in vain. As she began to shut the door, something caught her eye. Ayesha's only memory of her father, the same black and white picture, lay tattered at the doorstep.

2

Letters

At midnight, she lay in her bed, awake, reading the letter for the sixth time. The candle by the side of her bed lit every line of the letter written in Urdu. With each word she read, her face glowed with joy. She read till her eyes grew sore, until she memorized the words that would haunt her for many days to come.

She would read it again, Iyra promised herself before carefully folding the four-page letter. She cautiously added it to her treasure of the other fifteen letters that she hid under her bed.

That night, she slept peacefully; just like she would after every letter. But she knew it was not something long-lasting. The wait for the next letter would bring back anxiety and sleeplessness soon.

Letters from Ali were a combination of peace and pain. She lived with his promises and letters since he had left two years ago. They first met when Iyra was graduating in arts.

Ali worked at a stationery shop opposite her college.

Iyra clearly remembered the day they first met. That day, she had forgotten to carry her notebook and went to the shop to buy a new one. In the rush for her classes, she quickly grabbed a notebook with a white cover from a shelf. Nervously waiting at the cash counter, she frisked through her bag for coins.

Iyra pushed through a group of students to pay. It was then that she caught Ali's eyes at her. She swiftly looked away, paid for the notebook, and ran to her classes.

As her visit to the shop became regular, their conversations began. They would talk about the weather, the latest movies, and Bollywood songs. They met along the banks of the river that flowed parallel to Iyra's college. Young couples in college and school uniforms would often be spotted around the boulevard that remained less crowded. It was a favourite haunt for young lovers.

Iyra and Ali sat under the shade of a *chinar* tree on a pier. It was a place away from the hustle and bustle of the city. It was a place where they felt safe from the eyes of the world. They held hands silently watching the placid river flow with colourful wooden houseboats dotting its borders.

"I have walked along this river right from my childhood," Ali spoke as he held her hand. "I have seen the world around it change... I could never imagine, that one day, my world would also change here."

Iyra smiled, resting her head on his shoulder. "I hope this dream doesn't vanish... my whole world is here," she replied softly.

They spent most of the time in silence and promised to meet again at the same spot. She bunked classes; Ali skipped work. They would spend the whole day at a garden along a famous lake in the city, sitting by the flowers, guarded by lofty mountains and open skies. The *shikara*[2] steered through the calm lake when Ali proposed to her for marriage. Rowing through the dale of yellow lotus, they promised to be together till they last.

When they parted that day at the bus stop along the banks of the lake, Iyra felt something snap inside her. She stood there amidst the crowd of commuters. Her eyes followed Ali walking through the parked buses and rushing passengers. He disappeared from her sight.

For the following two weeks, no news came from Ali. Iyra waited; sometimes outside his shop, at other times in the park where they often met.

One day as she headed home from her college, she met Ali's colleague.

"Ali asked me to give this to you," the young boy said as he handed over a white wrinkled envelope to Iyra.

"Where is he and how is he?"

"Read the letter," the boy said, waving her goodbye.

Waiting to get home to read the letter meant further delay and anxiousness. Iyra ran to a nearby park, sat under a tree and began to read:

I don't know where to begin, Ali wrote in black ink.

I know you have many questions to ask. I don't know if, after reading this letter, you would want to carry on with our relationship. But I can't hide the truth from you any further.

---

[2] Flat-bottomed boat

Iyra, I have joined the cause of freedom and have been a part of an organization for two months. I did not have the courage to tell you this so far for the fear of losing you. But now, I think it is the right time for you to know.

I know this is shocking for you and I apologize for not having said anything so far. Life has not been the same for me. I brush with death each passing day. The only thing that has not changed is my feelings for you.

Time does not allow me to write a long letter. But I want to assure you that you would be the first and last person in my life. I stand by every promise I made, every word I said to you.

The decision to go ahead with this relationship lies with you. Be wary of the struggle and pain it would bring.

If I don't get any reply to this letter, I would understand you chose a different life.

Remember, I will always be with you."

Iyra felt a stab in her heart as she held the letter close to her chest. Her vision grew blurry. She could hardly see the world around her. She never imagined her life would take such a turn. She read the letter repeatedly.

The rays of the setting sun dimmed her thin figure under the tree. She noticed she was alone in the park.

It was already dark when she reached home. She walked straight to her room, every word in the letter echoing in her head. She spent the night wondering about

Ali. She worried for his life and about the life she was going to live now.

With the first rays of the rising sun, she wrote to Ali.

Ali,

Remember the day you made a promise to me to bring me happiness? The day, which was all bright, with flowers and lotus around?

I knew every word you said was true, but I also knew that life shall not always be roses.

To love doesn't meet to float in happiness and dance in blossoms. Love means living in sacrifice with each breath. And I am ready for it.

I will wait till you come back, whenever it may be...

She carefully folded the letter and slipped it into a white envelope. Iyra thought of writing the address at the post office before mailing it. She hid it in a small pocket of the bag she carried to college. She posted the letter on her way to college the next day.

Iyra began to spend her time writing and re-writing letters to Ali, and waiting for the right time to leave home to mail them.

Two years passed. The correspondence didn't stop. They wrote letters filled with love, hope and tears. At the end of every letter Iyra would ask the same question,

"When will you come back?" But she never got an answer.

With time, Iyra's longing for Ali only grew stronger. She would often visit their meeting spots, scribbling her name with Ali's, jotting down dates, and hoping that soon they will meet at the same place again. She dreamt of visiting all the beautiful places and Mughal gardens, about going for *shikara* rides, and chatting under the mighty *chinar* trees.

Every letter that she received gave her the strength to wait longer even though there was a constant fear of losing Ali to the bullets. She often woke up screaming from her sleep after a bad dream. Sometimes, she would see Ali dead, drenched in blood; at other times she saw him running into a wild jungle as Iyra chased him.

The struggle for Iyra got harder when her family announced their marriage plans for her.

"I am not ready for marriage yet. I need time to study further," she told her father.

"There is no reason for you to say no. You are done with your education and we cannot support you further with that."

"But I need time. I cannot marry just anyone."

Before Iyra could elaborate, she was told her engagement was fixed for the following month. She was to marry a businessman, who was also her distant relative.

Iyra grew numb. She thought of telling the truth to her family, *but who would believe in a relation of letters?* she told herself.

She would face questions to which she had no answers.

Iyra quietly went to her room, choked by her emotions. Unable to take the burden of the situation alone, she started writing to Ali:

The time for the test of your promise has come. My family has planned my engagement next month.

I am in no position to talk about you unless you come forward. Your letters won't convince them of your commitment.

You have one week to decide. I shall meet you in the same park the same day next week.

I hope to see you.

This was the last letter she wrote. Ali did not write back either. The whole week passed in anxiousness and thoughts of losing Ali. She had put her trust in him for two years, but now it seemed like she was losing the battle. All those days, she kept herself going by reminding herself of their beautiful moments together and reading the letters repeatedly.

That morning, Iyra reached their meeting spot by nine. She grabbed a piece of bread and a glass of water to keep herself from giving into the fatigue.

Her mind was blank. She felt nothing. Her future looked dark to her.

She walked into the park and sat near the tree where she had scribbled their names. She rubbed her hand over the names. And leaned over it.

Her thoughts moved back to their days together, their meetings, and their parting. She thought of her family who loved her and wanted to see her happy.

She watched the visitors coming to the park and envied couples spending happy times together as she longed for a moment of happiness with her beloved.

Every minute seemed to be an hour for her.

The scorching sun and heat did not deter her spirit. Exhausted from waiting, she began to fall asleep under the tree. She dreamed of Ali holding her hand and taking her along. They walked past the lake, over the fallen flowers from the almond trees, and past the mountains.

A gentle touch on her feet stirred her awake. She found herself staring into dark brown eyes.

It was not Ali. She stepped aside in defence. Her heart raced and her mouth became dry.

"Don't get scared of me. I have come to meet you," the man told her. She scanned the tall figure of the man standing in front of her. She hadn't seen him before.

"Who are you and what do you want from me?" Iyra asked, looking at his dark hair falling on his forehead. His face looked worn out. His eyes looked tired. He wore a black *pheran*[3].

---

[3] Long, lose garment worn in winter in Kashmir

"I was the one who wrote letters to you," he said, lowering his gaze as he spoke in a broken voice.

Iyra felt as if she was hit by a huge stone. Her head began to spin, her thoughts unable to settle.

Zain told her; he was Ali's friend who had joined a militant organization with him.

Ali would often speak to him about Iyra. "He loved you truly and wanted to marry you."

"But I want to see him. Where is Ali? Why are you here?" Iyra repeated as tears ran down her cheeks.

"Ali had plans to get back home and send a marriage proposal to your family," Zain told her.

"Ali had got you gifts and wished to surprise you on your birthday. But …

… but, he was killed … two months after he joined the fight.

The day he was buried, I received your letter. Reading your words, I knew it would be devastating to tell you the truth, so I wrote you back.

"Your letters brought back the lost spirit in me. I had never thought I would ever change like this..."

Zain confessed that he had fallen in love with her even though he had never seen her except for a few pictures she had sent to Ali.

"I still have your pictures with me," Zain fished his pocket for Iyra's picture where she posed on a sofa in a white dress. She had gotten the picture clicked from a nearby photo studio so she could send it to Ali.

Iyra stood frozen. The whole world was whirling around her. Her legs trembled. She leaned against the tree where her name was written with Ali's. As Zain spoke, she hid her face in her hands and wept.

"I don't know what your decision would be but I will always love you. I want to be with you alone. I have come back for you, just for you."

Iyra's tears didn't cease. Every word from Zain ripped her heart. She wanted to say many things and ask a lot of questions, but couldn't utter a single word.

Zain held her hand, asking her to forgive him for keeping the truth under wraps for such a long time.

"I did not want to break your heart. I wanted to give you a life..."

Iyra looked into his eyes, which were welled up with tears. The moment seemed to stop. She thought about Ali, every word of the letters haunting her. Her heart collapsed.

Zain took out all the letters written by Iyra that he had preserved.

She touched the love-soaked letters and a faint smile flickered on her lips.

3

The Spinning Wheel

It was his first visit home that year. Usman was excited to see autumn turn the *chinar* leaves golden along the boulevard of the river. His house stood close by, in a lane that connected the bund to the main road.

It was a congested locality with residential houses and shops jostling for space.

That evening, he left home for a stroll along the river, hoping to catch the sunset. As he walked a few metres ahead, his eyes caught the sight of a house at the corner of the lane. The house was being pulled down. Its belongings—furniture, utensils etc.—were being dumped on the road alongwith the rubble from the house.

In the growing pile of debris, he noticed a spinning wheel swathed in dust and mud.

It was the same spinning wheel that connected him to the house which was now in ruins.

The first time Usman stepped into that house was when he was a ten-year-old. That winter, he enjoyed playing cricket on the street with his friends in the neighbourhood. During the game, the batter flung the ball into the air. It landed somewhere in the compound of the house.

Usman ran to chase the ball. He banged open the iron door. The sight of a middle-aged woman, sitting on the veranda, caught his eyes. She sat on a small piece of rug, her eyes and hands following the movements of a spinning wheel. She was so absorbed in her work that she failed to notice his presence.

Usman was so awed that he didn't know how to react. He had never come across something like this before. As he stood still at a distance, his eyes followed every motion of the wheel. The voice of his friend down the street calling his name interrupted him. He quickly got the ball amid the bushes and ran at a pace Sarah's eye couldn't follow.

That night before going to sleep, Usman thought about the wheel. He felt the urge to touch it once. He decided to visit the woman again. The following day, around the same time, Usman walked out of his house and headed straight to Sarah's home. He did not know how to introduce himself, but was sure the woman wouldn't mind letting him in. He knocked on the wooden door. Sarah opened, smiling at Usman. "What brings you here again, boy," she asked softly. She wore a clean set of clothes and covered her head with a scarf. Her scarf did not hide the strands of her grey hair.

"I am Usman. I live a few houses down the road. Can I see the wooden wheel that you have?" Sarah broke into a light laugh. Without asking him further questions, she asked him to follow her.

She guided him through a narrow corridor that appeared to have been painted years back. There were rooms on both sides of it. A rundown staircase led to the upper storey. Usman followed Sarah into the kitchen. His eyes immediately caught the spinning wheel. Sarah sat near the window with the wheel in front of her. Usman sat next to her.

She began to spin cotton on the wheel into thin threads. She slowly showed Usman how it worked and even gave him a chance to play around with it. Usman warmed up to her company. She gave him cookies and sweets to eat. When it was almost afternoon, he left for home.

His visits to Sarah became regular. On every visit, she began to tell him a story and that kept him hooked even more. She told him about a fifteen-year-old boy, Zafar, who loved playing cricket like him.

"He was famous for his bowling skills and wanted to be a cricketer," she told Usman one day as he sat by the window of her kitchen. Usman's mind began to imagine a boy like him running to pitch the ball at the batter.

"So, did he become one?" Usman asked excitedly.

"One afternoon, while his mother went out to call him for lunch, he was nowhere to be seen," she told him. She went everywhere to find him, but he did not return ..." Sarah added.

"She still looks out for him during lunchtime every day for the past twelve years."

Another story was about an eighteen-year-old Masood who was a topper in his class.

"He was a science nerd and wished to innovate something that could solve the problem of power cuts in poor families. One day, he went to school and did not return," Sarah told him during one of his visits.

His books and school bag were found on the school premises. They are intact even after fourteen years, she told him.

It was, however, the story of nineteen-year-old Azhar that moved Usman to tears. As Sarah told him about his love for flying kites and his passion for doing community service, he felt shame for his lack of both.

"When he was hit by a stray bullet while flying his hand-made kite along the river, he fell to the ground but kept holding tightly onto his kite," she spoke as her eyes followed the motions of the spinning wheel.

Sarah told him the kite has been preserved, and remains untouched for eleven years.

Usman grew interested in stories. With the love of the spinning wheel, he began to fall in love with the boys in the stories. He thought about them often and asked Sarah to tell him more stories. She would tell the tales with a smiling face and soaked in real emotion.

After a year, Usman was sent to a school in another city and his visits to the house stopped. But every time he came home, he would visit Sarah. As he grew older, he began to wonder why Sarah always lived alone. Why he never saw her children, husband, or any family member. He was surprised by his own lack of emotion and attention towards the woman who loved him and showed him so much compassion.

One day Usman, who was now a seventeen-year-old, thought of asking Sarah about her family. He was on a week's holiday. He walked to her house. Despite a few knocks on the door, no one responded. He found the door open. Hesitantly, he entered and walked down the dark hallway. He heard some movements in one of the rooms along the corridor. Usman walked towards it and slowly opened the door. It was a small room painted in green. The room was better furnished than the others. In a corner, he saw Sarah with her back to him. A huge metal trunk stood in front of her. The trunk was full of some items which Usman could not see clearly.

Slowly, she took a kite, partly tattered, out of the trunk and put it aside. Then came a school bag, cricket bat and ball. One by one she took out photographs of three boys with their names written at the bottom: Zafar, Masood, and Azhar.

Usman was taken aback. He could not hold back his tears. He felt ashamed for his insensitivity. Pain stabbed him. Sarah had been living with the memories of her sons. He could not bear the sight anymore and left. He cried all his way back home. After a few months, he heard Sarah's husband had also died of cancer many years back.

Sarah lived alone for years. Usman stopped visiting her. His sense of remorse would not allow him to face her.

But every time he passed by her house, his eyes would well up.

Three years since his last visit, Usman now stood outside her house while it was being demolished. He ran around to ask about Sarah. He was told that she was found dead in her sleep few months back with all the remains of her sons by her side. She slept with them every night, a neighbour told him.

The house was sold off by her brother. The new owner planned to construct commercial structure there. But what happened to those kites, books, and photos?

Usman rushed inside the house that was being demolished. He searched every room, but found nothing. Even the trunk was missing. Feeling hopeless, he sat at the same spot in the kitchen where Sarah told him stories. He felt her fingers caress his cheek; her sweet voice rang in his ears. He felt her presence all around. Unable to bear the pain, he walked out.

Outside, the pile of rubble was growing as the house came down. Usman delved into the pile and dug out the spinning wheel, the only memory he now had of Sarah. He dusted it with his hand and hugged it close.

4

Gone Forever

Every evening, at around 8 pm, they would sit in a corner of the kitchen on a rug.

Maira would teach Aleem how to read and write.

She never missed giving him classes. Routinely, after finishing her homework, she would gather her old books, and list out things to teach him. Even during cold winter evenings when the power supply would be snapped for hours, she would sit by the candlelight to teach him how to write his name.

Aleem was about nineteen years old. Maira was a second-standard student.

Aleem was introduced into the family when Maira's mother got sick with a skin disease and needed help with household chores. He was the son of a farmer who once worked as a gardener at their place. Poverty kept Aleem, who spent most of his childhood helping his father in the fields, illiterate. He also worked as a manual labourer before starting to work as a domestic help at Maira's house.

His arrival made Maira happy. She now had more time to spend with her mother. Aleem was paid well for his work. He was provided with a separate room, a few sets of clothes, and a radio for his entertainment.

Aleem immediately took responsibility for the household work. He would start his day at six in the morning, make everyone breakfast, lay the table, and pack

Maira's lunch. By 8 am, he would carry Maira's bag and accompany her to the bus stop. He would wait with her till the bus arrived.

During his free time, Aleem would listen to Bollywood songs on the radio. Mithun Chakraborty was his favourite actor. He pasted his pictures on the mirror in his room and would often try to imitate his hairstyle and gestures. He curiously waited for his movies on the local channels.

But Aleem never dreamt of acting like many of the youth of his time. In his heart, he had a silent wish of opening a free school in his village so that others like him could have a better future.

He liked to see Maira go to school every day and would wave at children in the bus. When Maira did her homework, Aleem would flip through the pages of her textbooks. He would look at the colourful pictures, trying to make sense of the lessons.

Touched by his love for education, Maira decided to teach Aleem and at least make him literate. She taught him every day, took his exams, and promoted him to 'classes.'

The first time Aleem wrote his name, he was overjoyed. He made a semolina dish for the family and bought Maira chocolates.

However, the happy moments did not last long. Everything changed for Maira and her family when Aleem went missing.

That day he had left home to buy groceries from the local market. When he did not return in two hours, Shamim, Maira's father, went around the market to look for him. He asked the shopkeepers and the grocer but was unsuccessful in getting any information about Aleem.

As the sun began to set, the worry of the family grew. Shamim had no option but to inform Aleem's father, Razaaq.

The elderly man went to every house to find his lone son. He asked his friends and relatives to check if Aleem was with them. But he was neither seen nor heard of anywhere. It was as if he had disappeared into the thin air!

Maira and her family missed Aleem. No one was hired to replace him. His room remained untouched. His pair of jeans and T-shirt hung from the peg behind the door. The trunk where he kept his belongings was unmoved from its place. A bottle of shampoo, comb, a local perfume, and hair gel stood on top of it as he used it as a dressing table.

The money saved for his family was wrapped in a handkerchief kept under a pile of clothes.

He had rolled his mattress, cleaned the room, and left. The posters of Mithun stared from the abandoned mirror.

Maira preserved the books she taught him, sure that he would come back soon.

A year passed.

Shamim continued to search for Aleem through different sources. He paid regular visits to Razaaq who had lost his health because of all of this.

With Aleem long gone and two married daughters, there was no one to look after him and his wife.

However, the aging couple still had hope of seeing Aleem come back someday.

All that had belonged to him was well preserved by his family.

The last time he had met his family, Aleem looked content with his work. He had promised to send his parents for Haj for which he had been saving money.

But Razaaq and his wife now had only one wish … to see their son.

On his routine visit to Razaaq's place, about two years past Aleem's disappearance, Shamim saw a police vehicle outside his house.

Is there any news about Aleem? He wondered as he quickened his pace towards the two-storey mud house.

He found the door wide open and stepped inside.

"What is happening here?" Shamim asked, "Why do we have police here?"

Razaaq and his wife sat in a corner of the room with two police officers facing them.

They informed him that Aleem's dead body has been found in a forest.

"We want you to come in and identify him. For now, his body is at the morgue beside the police control room," a police constable informed Shamim.

Shamim did not know how to respond. His eyes went straight to Razaaq and his wife who were in shock.

Aleem's smiling face flashed before Shamim's eyes. His mind replayed the days when he lived with them. Never had he showed any signs of being a militant or reflected any inclination towards the freedom movement.

What happened to Aleem was a question left unanswered.

But for this mystery to end, they had to follow what the police said.

The twenty-minute journey in the police van was painfully long. Shamim sat next to Razaaq, silently praying for Aleem's well-being. Now they wished the wait for him would not end.

They did not exchange a word all the way. Aleem's thoughts engaged their minds.

They stared at the old building of the police control room as the van came to a halt.

Is my son dead inside? Razaaq thought to himself.

He stood still, his eyes on the building as Shamim tried to get him out of the van.

A police constable directed them inside, where they had to walk through the dark corridors until they came to a huge iron door.

Shamim's heart plunged at the creak of the morgue door.

It took them a few minutes to note a stretcher lying amid the dark and cold room. They walked slowly, guided by the light of the single window.

They stood numb, looking at the body covered in white cloth.

Slowly, Shamim gathered the strength to slip off the cloth over the face.

Aleem lay there, silent, sleeping.

Razaaq grabbed his arm, trying to wake him up.

He rubbed his hand over his face, his hair, and his legs. He didn't cry, he didn't say a word. He touched his son like he was meeting him after ages.

Shamim watched as the helpless father repeatedly kissed his son.

"Where have you been?" Razaaq said as he held him in his arms.

"I knew you would come back, but now why don't you speak to me?"

Shamim held Razaaq and hugged him. The two cried as they stood in the darkness of the mortuary next to Aleem, who was dressed in clothes that Shamim had bought him on last Eid he was with the family.

A police constable interrupted them.

"We found a bag near his body. You can keep it," he said as he handed over the bag to Shamim.

Curious to find any clue about what had happened to Aleem, he unzipped the bag.

But what he saw surprised him.

There were notebooks where he wrote his Mathematics and English lessons. He had some pencils and erasers in a small pocket beside one of Maira's old textbooks.

As he fished into another pocket, he found an envelope.

Shamim's family photo was carefully wrapped in a piece of paper. Aleem had carried it along.

And then he found another picture, that of Mithun.

5

The Graveyard Garden

Sam always dreamt of having his own garden. His house, standing two storeys tall on the road, shared walls with the neighbouring buildings. The windows on two sides looked over the main street. Much to his disappointment, there was no space that could be converted into a garden.

Back in school, he enjoyed gardening during his hobby class. He had planted colourful flowers in multi-coloured pots. He kept them lined up on the window sill and tended to them every day. He remembered the names of many flowers and could identity about fifty different kinds of plants.

One Sunday, when he was on his way to the market, an abandoned plot of land caught his sight in a lane next to his house. He noticed three epitaphs with flowers growing around them. Narcissus and lilies were neatly growing with some green shrubs. Sam had never come across anything like this before. The sight was new to him and piqued his interest. He got an idea—of converting the place into a garden.

The thought of the floral graveyard occupied his mind all the way back home. In his head, he was planning a garden he would make all by himself.

There were several graves that did not have flowers. Sam, eleven-year-old, wished to turn it into a garden where he could play anytime.

The whole thought brought him endless joy. Being the only child in the family, Sam was always battling his loneliness. He did not have friends either, except at school. He always wished for a sibling or a friend to play with after his school hours and on his holidays. But now he had something wonderful to do, he told himself.

It did not take too much thought to execute what he had planned. All he had to do was get his gardening set from school. He knew he could do gardening only on Sundays when his school was off and his parents would sleep till late.

So, on the following Sunday, he woke up at 6 am. He got dressed in his pair of shorts and a T-shirt. For a better grip for his feet, he wore his sneakers. He quietly slipped through his room into the corridor and unlocked the main door that opened on the road itself.

He heaved a sigh of relief to see the street deserted. He walked quickly to reach the place. He opened the small iron gate and stood still, looking at the whole piece of land in front of him. He saw new and old graves. But flowers decorated only two. He sat down for a while to think where to start.

His first thought was to decorate the old grave that looked untidy. He did not read what was written on the epitaphs. That just didn't interest him. He wanted to make the place his own.

So, he began his work. He went to the grave in the farthest corner. It was hidden by wild grass. Before he began planting flowers, there was a task of preparing the soil. He began pulling out the wild grass from its roots. It took him no more than half an hour before he cleared the grass around the whole grave. He rested for a while as he thought about the breadth of the flower bed he intended to make.

With a showel he put a mark around the grave and began to dig soil within. By the time he dug the soil for sowing plants, it was time for him to go. Sam knew beforehand that he could not fulfil the task in a single session. He left the soil ready to be planted with flowers.

The rest of his day was spent sitting by the window of his room on the second storey. He thought of different types of flowers he wanted to plant. There was no issue in getting seeds as they were provided for free at his school. While he thought of all this, a boy in the neighbourhood caught his eye. His house was two houses away. The boy was painting flowers on a big canvas. Sam was awed. The boy looked his age, but he had never seen him before. Sam kept track of his work as he painted white lotuses. But shortly after, the boy was called inside by his mother.

The next day at school was a hard day for Sam. He could not get away from the thought of his garden. He kept wondering all the time, how he could make the place unique.

He stuffed his bag with flower seeds during recess time.

The following Sunday brought the joy of planting the seeds and watering them. He prepared the soil around another grave as well.

That day he spent a lot of time in his room watching the boy paint. He tried to whistle to him so that he could wave 'hello.' The boy did look at him and both smiled. Sam's off days were now happier and more joyful. Every Sunday morning, he would do some gardening at the graveyard where flowers had begun to bloom. He loved to see the white, pink, and mauve flowers, and red roses grow. In the afternoon, he would watch the boy paint. They exchanged warm, friendly glances, gestures, and smiles.

Sam wanted to tell the boy about his passion for gardening. He wanted to meet him and take him to his garden.

He decided to visit him on the next day off. He thought of buying him a gift, a colour box.

Throughout that week, Sam looked forward to meeting his 'friend.'

It was one of the most joyful mornings for Sam that Sunday. He made a quick visit to his garden to water the flowers and headed back home. He had a bath and got ready. After breakfast, he told his parents about the boy and that he planned to meet him.

Sam left home after lunch with the thought of buying some gifts for his friend. He had to walk about half a kilometre to reach the stationary shop. Very thoughtfully, he chose a twenty-four-piece colour box for him.

While he waited at the cash counter to make the payment, he heard some commotion around him in the market. A huge mob of people passed by the shop, shouting slogans. The police arrived soon after. It quickly escalated to stone-pelting and teargas shelling.

The shopkeeper tried to pull down the shutter, but Sam slipped through the gap and ran. Such sights were not new to his areas where protests were common. In all this commotion, all Sam could think of was to head straight to his friend's place and be safe there, sitting with him. Carrying the box of colours that he grabbed in a hurry, he ran as fast he could. Suddenly, he felt something hit his head and he fell to the ground.

Sam felt everything spinning around, but kept his grip on the box.

He lay motionless on the hospital bed as doctors tried to save him, but in vain. The shell had inflicted an internal injury to his brain. His parents lost their only son who had just begun to live life.

Amid wails and moans, Sam was taken for burial to the graveyard he converted into a 'garden'. The entire locality was drowned in grief. He was buried between flowers and their fragrance. No one knew it was Sam who brought life to this abandoned piece of land.

Late in the evening that day, when the sun was almost set and everyone had returned home, Sam's 'friend', Azeem, came walking to the graveyard. Azeem wanted to make friends with Sam and wished to gift him the portrait that he had painted.

He sat by his grave and wept. He remembered the day when he had seen him for the first time tending the plants at the graveyard while on a morning walk with his father.

That was the moment he decided to be his friend. But now, his friend was gone forever. Azeem put the painting he had made on Sam's grave. He walked into the darkness of the night, promising himself to take care of his friend's garden forever.

6

Fridays

Hamaad loved Fridays. That day, his school would finish early, allowing him to join his friends for prayers at a nearby mosque. While getting back home, he enjoyed resting by the window of his room and watching pigeons gather in big numbers in the compound of a shrine opposite his house.

It was a small shrine that Hamaad had grown up seeing. He passed by it every day, casually, without saying any prayer or making a wish. He never thought of it as being 'special'. For him, it was just a small green structure that stood overshadowed by other buildings and houses.

He did not know what lay inside the cemented fence enclosing the shrine. The small holes in the paving gave a limited glimpse of the inside. The only things of interest for him were the pigeons in the shades of grey, white, and brown, flying in and out of the shrine to peck at grains.

One Friday, Hamaad sat by the window as usual. He was back from his school and had finished his prayers. He gazed at the pigeons.

It was then that a young woman getting off a local bus caught his attention. She wore a casual grey salwar kameez, matched with a white headscarf. After paying the bus fare, she walked towards the shrine. Hamaad was surprised when he saw her stop at the 'holy place'. She leaned her head against the green walls, peeking through the fence holes. She covered her face with her hands as she wept. No one stopped to console her.

Hamaad observed curiously as the woman held out her scarf and tore its corner. She kissed it with closed eyes, whispering something under her breath. She then tied a knot on the fence with the piece of her scarf.

Before she left, she kissed the tied knot. She walked, and walked.

Hamaad's eyes followed her until she disappeared. He wondered why she had come to an abandoned shrine; what wish she made.

From that day, every morning, thirteen-year-old Hamaad would peep through the window to see the white knot. It was untouched, unmoved. *Was the woman's wish granted?* he wondered to himself.

The following Friday, Hamaad waited for the woman. He hoped she would untie the knot, sure that her wish would be granted. The woman arrived, but only to pray. She again kissed the knot and left.

It was then that a frail elderly woman appeared from a small lane adjacent to the shrine.

Her traditional burqa hid her face, and she carried a plastic bag in her hands. At the iron gate of the shrine, she fed the bag full of grains to the pigeons. She sat down on the dirty road and leaned against the door.

As she raised her hands in prayer, she wept. Hamaad felt a deep pain to see the old woman crying. He saw her fumbling with her burqa and pulling a thread off its hem.

She closed her teary eyes while she tied the thread into a knot on the handle of the door. He watched as her delicate figure vanished into the narrow lane.

That night before going to sleep, Hamaad could not resist looking through the window. The shrine was draped in the darkness of the night. The threads were not visible to him.

Every Friday added knots to the shrine as more people paid a visit. They would cry, pray, tie the knot, and leave. Except for the first woman, no one came back.

Never had Hamaad seen people gather at the shrine like now. His curiosity grew with each passing day as the number of threads and wishes increased. His focus was now on the threads that embellished the fence and the iron door. The knots stood there, enduring vagaries of weather.

Time passed, and Hamaad left Kashmir to pursue his further education. That shrine remained close to his heart, putting many questions before him. On his first visit home as a twenty-one-year-old man, he decided to visit the shrine.

He left his home alone, and walked across the road. For the first time in his life, he had gone so close to it. He touched its walls, its tainted iron gate and the threads that still stood there. He began to look inside through the gaps in the fence. What he saw brought him surprise.

An old derelict grave caught his eyes first. Its epitaph was bare, with no inscription. It was covered by a green cloth with verses of Quran written in gold thread. He could not read what was written on it. The dust of time had gathered over it and bugs had made small holes into it. There were bushes and shrubs growing wildly around the grave. It appeared not to have been cleaned for years.

Hamaad stood there, his thoughts going to people who pinned hopes on a deserted shrine.

That night Hamaad missed sleep. That white knot still lingered in his mind.

The Friday that followed his stay at home, he stood near the window as always. He had been missing the birds, the people, and the ritual of tying knots. The shrine was now visited by a crowd, mostly youth.

But he was waiting for that first woman who kept coming back. He wanted to talk to her, ask her why she had come to the shrine that day, years back. He wanted to know why she wept every Friday. He would ask her the reason she tied the knot and why it still stood there.

Hamaad's vacation after finishing college was almost coming to a close. He was scheduled to fly back soon.

But this time, he would not leave without getting his answers. It was his last Friday at home, Hamaad waited for the woman to come. This time, she did not return.

He walked to the shrine, thinking he might have missed seeing her. He waited till it was almost dark. He walked a few meters and stopped near a tea stall. He wondered how all these years the shrine grabbed his attention while his eyes skipped the presence of a tea seller.

An old man dressed in traditional *pheran* stood behind the wooden cart. His presence was diluted by the row of stainless-steel glasses and pile of locally baked puffs.

The tea seller stood up from his stool assuming he had a customer.

"Shall I make you a cup of chai?" the man asked.

"Actually, I have come over to ask you something."

"Go ahead," the man said.

Hamaad asked him if he knew the woman who came to the shrine all these past years.

"She was the first one I saw visit the shrine."

He described the woman's gloomy face, her blue scarf with white flowers that had faded with time and her tearful visit to the shrine every Friday. "Oh, I think you are referring to Masooda. She would often come to have tea here," the tea seller replied.

Masooda lived in a nearby town. She had been visiting the shrine after her son went missing and it was then that she had come to tie the knot as she held hopes on anything that looked or appeared to be holy and divine.

The man told Hamaad that the holy place kept her spirits and hope up until the day she discovered her son was no more.

"It was just three days back that his body was found … after eight years of waiting." "Now she doesn't need to come here anymore."

Hamaad was shocked. He could not say a word. His heart grew heavy, his eyes became sore. Without bidding goodbye to the tea seller, he walked silently towards the shrine as the sun began to set.

At the shrine, he began to sift through the rotten clutter of multi-coloured knots until he found the white knot that Masooda had tied. Hamaad untied it, held it tight in his fist and walked into the darkness of the night.

7

Poetry for the Dead

Autumn had begun to set in. The *chinar* trees had turned gold. Leaves flaked from poplars. The streams were drying slowly as they waited for the snow to replenish them the next season.

Forty-eight-year-old Ahad noted a dip in the number of visitors as the vehicles passing by his shop declined. The road where his shop stood led to the famous tourist spots in the valley.

Ahad would spend hours looking at the road as he had many days free from work. He sat amid huge slabs of stones which he turned into epitaphs for the graves. He inscribed them with the names and dates of the dead. People from across the valley were his customers. He made a living every time someone died; the rest of the time he was free.

Ahad would spend his free time helping his wife Zaina prepare for the coming winter. They stacked the firewood, burned dry leaves to prepare charcoal, and dried vegetables in the sun.

They lived in a two-roomed house which he built over eight years with his meagre income. The family mostly survived on the vegetables they grew in their small lawn, nurtured by the couple themselves.

Their sixteen-year-old son, Aftab, would spend his time mostly at school or playing cricket in the nearby street.

Aftab was never asked to take the burden of household chores. His parents wished him to pursue studies and enjoy his days of youth.

Despite fighting to meet their ends, the small family lived peacefully.

One winter morning, as Ahad was still struggling to get out of the bed, he heard some commotion outside. He waited for it to die, assuming that his neighbours must be fighting their usual brawl.

But when the voices got louder, he pulled away the tattered quilt, slipped into his long woollen *pheran* (long woollen cloak) and walked out of the house. He saw all his neighbours gathered on the street. They stood in a circle, looking curiously at something. He pushed through the crowd of about twenty men and women.

His neighbour, Afzal, held an Urdu newspaper in his hand. He was one of the few educated people in the locality and was reading the news to others around him. Ahad's eyes caught the picture of a bloodied body lying somewhere on the road. Another picture next to it showed the police throwing water on the blood-drenched street. Afzal read that there was a blast in the main city in which eleven people were killed.

It was a shock to the people who had never heard of such an incident before. Afzal read the news repeatedly as more people joined in. The whole locality gathered around the newspaper. Ahad returned home and told his wife about the news.

Amid the gloomy atmosphere of the morning, Ahad left for his usual day at the shop. His day was mostly spent with other shopkeepers discussing the news. It took a few days for the news to die down.

A few weeks later, a strong knock at the door at 6 am woke Ahad up from sleep. It was unusual to have any guests at that time. The sun had not risen yet and it was still dark outside.

He grabbed his torch from the bedside, wrapped a blanket around himself, and went to the door. Two young men stood waiting for him.

Without exchanging greetings, one of them blurted, "We need three epitaphs by the afternoon."

He slipped his hand into his pocket and handed a paper to Ahad.

"We want this to be written on the tombstones."

Ahad was left confused and shocked. Never has he received demands for more than one epitaph together. He wanted to ask about the tragedy, but then decided otherwise.

He left for work immediately and spent the whole day at work.

Late that evening, another man came to him.

"Salaam," the man dressed in a black *pheran* greeted Ahad.

"I have come from the city. I need a nice tombstone, but in black marble."

"But it would cost more," Ahad told him.

"There is no price for the life of an eighteen-year-old. This is just a stone over his young dead body."

The man handed over the details of the boy. His name, birth date, and the day of passing.

With each day, Ahad began getting more customers and he could no longer handle his business alone. Making epitaphs with his hand was hard work and he had no help.

He thought of engaging Aftab for etching the tombstones which would reduce his workload. As the schools were shut for the winter break, it would not affect his studies either, Ahad thought.

Aftab took a keen interest in designing the stone for the grave of the eighteen-year-old boy.

While he wrote his name, Abdullah, he wondered what the boy must have looked like. Did he like cricket like him, or was he fond of playing video games? He had not heard of anyone dying so young. He wanted to know how he died so soon, being born only eighteen years back …

Meanwhile the news about the growing violence and deaths from blasts and firing grew with each day. Men, women, and children were getting killed every day. The businesses began to suffer as many days were lost in shut-downs, but Ahad's business grew. He got about a hundred orders a week against the twenty that he would receive earlier.

As his income increased, Ahad's lifestyle got better.

He got a fridge for his home. He added one more room to the structure, and even got his house painted. However, happiness and peace of mind slowly began to disappear from his otherwise content home.

Ahad's heart broke when he was asked to make epitaphs of granite and marble for a nine-year-old boy and a seven-month-old baby who died after being hit by a stray bullet in its mother's arms.

Aftab spent the whole day making the epitaphs for these young children. He was so touched by their deaths; he began to write a few lines of his own.

"I will sleep in peace like in my mother's arms," he wrote on the tombstone of the seven-month-old baby. In his free time, Aftab started writing obituaries for the women and children. He carved them on the epitaphs and customers began to like them.

That summer, Aftab was spending more time at the shop. He missed school and would hardly go to play cricket. He failed in class for the first time.

His father tried to free him from work, but Aftab would keep coming back. He began to isolate himself within his room when he was not working.

While cleaning his room one day, Zaina flipped through his notebooks and saw obituaries written. He would spend the nights awake, singing melancholic songs. His sadness grew with each passing day. He no more laughed and joked with his parents, who were now anxious about his mental health.

They tried to talk to Aftab about his problem, but he kept quiet. He avoided spending time with his parents.

The day Ahad decided to take him to a psychiatrist, Aftab was busy making the epitaph for a seven-year-old boy who was killed by a stray teargas shell.

Ahad walked to him and asked him to shut the shop.

He was unmoved, engrossed in his work.

Ahad held him tight on his arm to grab his attention.

Aftab stared back with a blank face. Ahad tried to snatch the tool from his hand, but he tightly grabbed the marble slab, held it close to his chest and ran.

Ahad called out to him, ran after him as fast as his age allowed. But Aftab didn't even look back. He ran through the fields and into the wilds. Ahad shouted his name, called for help as his legs began to fail. He collapsed in the rice field.

Tears streamed from his eyes as Ahad saw his only son, carrying an epitaph, disappear into the wilderness.

8

Lost Dreams

Farhan had been out of his bed before the alarm rang. It was unusual as it would take several minutes of buzzing from the little blue time-piece by his bed-side to push him out from under the covers and get going.

However, today was a special day for the eighteen-year-old, and his excitement did not allow him to stay in bed. He was eager to rush to the school. It was the day when he would be awarded for his outstanding performance in basketball at the state level. He had already received many prizes and acknowledgements for his inter-school and inter-district competitions. But this one meant more as it opened doors for him to compete at the national level and then international.

He took a quick bath and started getting ready. Standing in front of the mirror, adjusting the red and grey tie over his white shirt, he saw himself as a rising basketball star. He prided himself silently for his achievements and promised within never to give up.

As he remained engrossed in his thought, his mother called him. It was his usual call for breakfast every morning.

He picked up his bag and went downstairs.

A feeling of accomplishment and pride ran through him as he sat between his parents.

"Farhan," his father said to him, "this is just the beginning. There is a lot more to achieve. Don't lose focus on your goal and never give up on hard work."

Farhan listened to his father as he spoke. His mother, Razia, ran her fingers through his hair in a loving gesture, her eyes shining with happiness and pride.

On that day, Farhan went to school on his own bike for the first time, which his father, Mohammad Iqbal gifted him. Though Iqbal worked as a clerk in a local bank, he made sure to fulfil all his son's wishes with his meagre income.

That afternoon, Iqbal and Razia sat proudly amongst the audience as the Minister of Sports and other dignitaries awarded their son for his achievement. The principal of the school gave a speech praising Farhan, and how he did his school proud.

After all the celebrations got over, Farhan went to the market before heading home. He purchased a box of sweets from a local bakery shop and headed to Saleem's house.

Saleem lived in the same locality as Farhan. He was about five years his senior. They knew each other after meeting at a local sports stadium while practising for basketball. Saleem was a champion a few years back. He had won several national and state-level awards for his achievements.

His name had appeared on TV, and newspapers carried his interviews. It was Saleem who coached Farhan during his initial years of playing basketball. They would spend their weekly off days at the sports stadium practising. Farhan credited Saleem for all his achievements.

Like Farhan, Saleem also dreamt of playing at the international level but his dream was shattered when he was hit on the leg by a tear gas shell. He was limited to a wheelchair for the rest of his life. He could never play basketball again after that. It took him months to come to terms with the fact, that he would never be able to walk again. He now wished to see his dream fulfilled through Farhan. He would mentor him and give him instructions about the game. He would watch him practice at the stadium every weekend to help him improve upon his performance.

Farhan's success brought tears in Saleem's eyes.

"You deserve this trophy more than me," Farhan told him as he sat next to Saleem. He ran his fingers across the golden globe and then his eyes went to the shelf where all his trophies rested.

"I want you to go beyond those trophies," Saleem told him.

"You have to make our people proud. You have to fulfil my dream too."

Farhan began to work harder on the sport. He would spend extra time practising after school.

Saleem was overjoyed when, a few months later, Farhan told him that he was selected for a national level tournament. The two hugged and wept with joy. They decided to celebrate the day. They went to their favourite restaurant overlooking the lake in the city centre to have their all-time favourite mutton dish with rice. This was followed by coffee at their pet coffee shop. They sat for hours together, discussing the game and how Farhan could make himself better at the sport. Saleem suggest him to get coaching outside the state to hone his skills.

That evening they returned home content with life. Saleem saw his vision being realized through Farhan who was now fancying the day he would fly out of his city to play his dream game.

That night Farhan was disturbed by a violent knock on his door. He got out of the bed and checked the time. It was 1:30 am. He went downstairs to answer the knock but saw his parents talking to someone at the door already. Security forces had cordoned their area and had information about militants being holed up in the locality. They were now questioning Iqbal.

"We have not seen anyone. We know nothing about any militant," Iqbal insisted.

However, a group of security men barged into their house and began to search every corner of the house.

Farhan and his parents watched silently as they opened their cupboards and threw their clothes on the floor, pulled the bedding off the beds, and turned the beds upside down, ransacked the sofa and decoration pieces, walked on the carpets with their boots and vandalized their kitchen in a bid to find the militants.

When they could not find anyone, they turned to Farhan and began to question him.

"What do you do?" an officer asked him.

"I am a student of class twelve," Farhan replied, adding that he wants to be a sports star.

"We want you to come with us."

Farhan looked at his parents not knowing how to answer.

"Don't worry, we will let you go soon."

Razia told the security forces that his son had nothing to do with militants.

"I don't know anything about the militants, sir," Farhan insisted trying to convince them of his innocence.

Without letting him speak further, a security person grabbed his arm and walked him out of the house. Farhan kept repeating that he was innocent but in vain.

Razia began to wail, begging at their feet that his son was innocent. Iqbal ran after them, pleading that they take him instead of his son. But their words made no impact. The couple stood wailing at their gate as they saw their son being pushed into an army truck and driven away.

Farhan was blindfolded all the way. He kept asking why he was being taken. He got no answers. He begged to let him go. But nothing worked.

After a long drive, a man held his arm and walked him into an unknown place. When Farhan opened his eyes, he saw himself between the four walls of a prison. His room had one small window for light. There was no bed, no other piece of furniture. It was all dark, empty, and cold. There were similar rooms next to his where people were lodged. Farhan could not understand what happened. He began to cry and scream, shouting that he was innocent. But no one came to his rescue.

The next morning Razia and Iqbal went to the nearby police station to file an FIR. They went to many army camps but couldn't find Farhan. When Saleem came to know of Farhan's arrest, he called his friend in the police for help.

Every day, Razia and Iqbal would set out for another district to search the police stations, camps, and interrogation centres. They would travel hours by bus to reach far off places.

Farhan didn't sleep for days. At first, he rejected food. Then he thought of his parents and gave in. After a week, a senior officer called him.

He was taken into a large room. He sat on a wooden chair facing another separated by a table. The room was barely lit except for the spotlight overhead. There were no windows. The officer sat opposite him.

"See, we do not want to hurt you. But you must tell us the truth," the officer said as he looked straight into Farhan's eyes.

Farhan saw fear, anger, and death. He did not know why he was facing all this. It took him a while to respond.

"I don't know anything about anyone. I live a normal life with my parents. Please let me go. My parents must be worried about me," Farhan began to cry.

The officer kept asking the same question repeatedly. Farhan's reply did not change.

"I think we need to use our hands to open his mouth," the officer pointed to a constable. He took hold of Farhan's arms, pushed him against the wall, and started kicking him in his abdomen. A strong wave of pain ran through Farhan's body. Before he could recover from the pang of sharp pain, he was hit on his arms, legs, back, and head. He could not gather where all it pained.

He screamed with helplessness, pleading his innocence, asking them to stop. But with every word of his, the beating got harder. They hit him till he could no longer speak.

When Farhan regained consciousness, he found himself back in his cell, lying on the bare floor. He couldn't move. Every inch of his body hurt. His chest ached with every breath he took. His legs were bruised. His jaw was wounded. His head was heavy and he couldn't move his neck. He somehow rested still against the wall, tears rolling down his eyes. He wanted to scream but could not. He had lost strength. He thought of his parents. Their helpless faces when he was taken from their home. He thought of Saleem and his promise to fulfil his dream. He dozed off.

The questioning and physical torture continued for weeks. Farhan grew used to it. There was no way he could answer them. His response was unchanged. Apart from offering prayers, he would spend his daydreaming of seeing his parents. Sometimes he wished an angel would come down and take him away... at other times, he planned to escape from the cell. He waited for his parents every day, hoping they would find him.

Farhan's parents, on the other hand, spent their days travelling, visiting prisons, army camps, meeting ministers, bureaucrats, and activists. Iqbal would often skip work. Saleem paid them a regular visit.

But now, they were slowly losing their health and strength. Razia was slipping into depression. Iqbal began to fall sick frequently. From dawn to dusk they waited.

Five years passed.

Farhan was busy with his prayer when a constable opened his door. It had been months since anyone came into his cell.

"The officer wants to meet you," he told Farhan.

He thought he would be questioned and tortured again. But now he was no more afraid of it.

Farhan walked across the long dark corridor leading to the room of the officer.

The officer sat on his chair with a pile of files open in front of him.

"Take a seat," he asked Farhan.

"It has been five years and all this time we have been trying to get information from you. During our investigation, we found out that you are innocent. So now we want you to go home," the officer told him.

Farhan's heart sank. He thought he was getting hallucinations and asked him to repeat what he said.

"You can go home now," the officer reassured him.

Farhan began to cry; he did not know how to respond. He was locked up without reason and now released suddenly.

He ran to his cell to get his prayer mat. He had nothing to carry along.

The moment he stepped out of the prison; the bright sunlight pinched his eyes. He had gotten used to the darkness. He looked at the sky, the birds, and the trees around. He looked at the earth and touched the soil. He cried and cried.

He headed straight for his home. On his way, he thought of all the things he would tell his parents. Farhan decided to leave with his parents for another city. He was not sure if he would ever be able to play basketball after the kind of torture his body had endured for years in prison. He had not heard from his parents all these years. He did not know how they were.

When he reached his home, he paused near the gate. He looked at his house in awe. He had missed home a lot, its comfort, its smell, and its feel.

He slowly opened the gate. He walked towards the main entrance of the house but saw that it was locked. He tried knocking, calling for his mother, but there was no answer. He took a closer look at the house and noticed that it had not been cleaned for a long time. He began to worry about his parents. He slowly went towards the backyard of the house.

What he saw shocked him. There were two graves next to each other with the names of his parents. They had died a few months apart. There was another grave. It was an open grave[4] but with an epitaph reading, "Farhan, we couldn't find you. We were told you have been killed. We still wait for you here. Come back to us and at least be on our side here, forever."

---

[4] Empty grave, waiting for the body to be buried

9

Story of a Cinema

Talib slowly opened his eyes as he gained consciousness. Everything around him looked blurry. He had to squint his eyes and blink frequently to see his surroundings. His mind was unable to recall instantly where he was. As he tried to move, his tied-up hands and feet brought back the memory of torture. He was in an interrogation centre, he remembered.

Talib, twenty-four-year-old, was left alone after he passed out during the interrogation. He immediately felt the need to drink water. But he could hardly speak a word or shout out for someone to give him some. He was tied to a chair and couldn't move. He reminded himself of his parents to keep himself alive. Tears ran down his cheeks as pain ignited every inch of his body.

He looked at the windows, the walls, the lights, and floor of the room. It was a place he knew, he visited and once loved. The window opposite his chair gave him the view of the main gate. It was dark-green and white, but had now begun to rust. It was through the same entrance that he would line up with his friends just a year back to watch movies at the famous cinema hall of the city, the Sizzlers.

Watching movies was one of the most common recreations for the people of Kashmir, which served as a shooting destination for scores of Bollywood block-busters. There were over fifteen movie theatres in the valley where all the latest Bollywood films would be screened. Locals would wait for Fridays for the release of the movies they planned to watch. The shows would screen till late into the night.

Talib, like many of the youth of his time, would curiously wait for the next Bollywood release and ensure that he watched the very first show. With his friends, he would keep the day free to watch the film. They would leave early from home and queue up at the gate of the Sizzlers. The movie lovers would rush early so as not to miss the 'first day, first show.'

Talib would dress in his trendy jeans and denim shirt. He would gel his hair to style it and wear his tan-coloured boots that his uncle in London had gifted him. He would finish his ensemble with his favourite perfume from Lomani. He would walk to his friend's place from where two of his friends would join him. They would often stop by a small departmental store to buy some potato wafers and drinks.

A long queue at the gate would lead to the cubicle of the ticket seller, Rehman. He was a man in his early fifties, with a strong build and long hair. Even at that age he followed fashion trends and dressed in style. He would often wear his brown leather jacket and chequered silk scarf matched with jeans. He had worked at the cinema for over thirty years to support his family of six.

Rehman would always follow the rules and make sure no one breached the queue.

The moment Talib got the tickets in his hand, he would rush inside through the green gate into the compound.

Wide cemented steps led into the movie theatre. There were small makeshift shops on either side of the steps selling snacks of all kinds: chocolates, biscuits, popcorns of different flavours, and cold drinks. A huge sliding glass door opened into a long corridor where posters of various movies were pasted on the walls.

On the right was the movie hall with a wide screen and maroon velvet chairs for the viewers.

Talib and company would always take the back row. He was a big fan of the Bollywood actor Amir Khan and never missed any of his films. He copied his attire, attitude, and hairstyle. After every new release of the actor, he would order a similar set of clothes for himself. The whole college would be awed at the style and attitude he carried.

He was the style icon whom other boys in his college followed. Watching his favourite actor on the big screen made Talib forget all the worries in life. He would carefully observe all his moves and memorize the dialogues. Once back home, he would recap the entire story to his mother mimicking the actor's expressions and dialogue.

Once the movie was over, they would hang around and often sit in a park and discuss the movie.

Life changed for Talib and youth like him when all the cinema halls were forced to be shut down by some militant organization. Many were bombed while announcements were made threatening visitors to cinema halls. Sizzlers was taken over by the security forces and converted into an interrogation centre where scores of youths were held. Their screams and voices now echoed the halls where once popular Bollywood songs reverberated. The cubicle where Rehman sold tickets was converted into a bunker.

Now, Talib was in the same cinema hall. But the reality was in contrast. He was not there to have fun with his friends. He was arrested for taking part in a protest after reports of mass rape in a village. The whole valley had observed a shut-down to demand justice for the incident that had taken place. Although he had not resorted to violence of any kind, he was bundled up with several others like him.

Talib was not caged within the same theatre. His only view of the world was the window opposite his chair that gave him sight of the main gate. All-day he would stare at the gate, waiting for someone to take him home, and remember his days of joy.

As he mostly kept his eyes on the gate, he once noticed a man knocking on it hysterically and leaving before coming back again after some time. No one opened the gate for him. His knocks were not even heard. Days passed; Talib remained tied to the same chair, though he was no more tortured. He was given some food once or twice a day and left alone in the room.

He kept his eyes on the gate. The man came every day, early in the morning, and left after it became dark. No one opened the door for him or said anything to him. He would come, knock on the door, and leave.

One day the gate opened to let a vehicle inside the compound. Talib caught the sight of the man. He was dressed in a kurta pyjama. He had a long beard and shabbily grown hair. At first, Talib did not recognize him, but as he heard the man shouting at the security forces, he recognized the voice as that of Rehman's.

Talib's heart broke. He did not understand why Rehman came there every day or why he was never attended to. Weeks passed; Talib kept waiting for Rehman to come and knock on the door. While it hurt him, it also gave him a sense of relief to see someone he knew every day.

One morning, Talib woke up to some sound in the room. He saw some security personnel standing in front of him.

"Our officer has asked us to let you go. But you must sign a paper assuring that you won't indulge in protests again," the security personnel told Talib.

He untied his hands and led him to another room. A senior officer sat on a wooden chair in front of a large table. He asked Talib to take a seat.

"See," the officer spoke to Talib, "we want a bright future for you boys. Concentrate on your education. Live peacefully. Do not force us to do all this."

He put a paper in front of him and asked him to sign.

Talib quickly took the pen and scratched his name. He asked if he could leave.

He left the room and walked into the large corridor where ragged posters of Bollywood films draped the walls. He looked at the posters of Amir Khan, Rajesh Khanna, Hema Malini, and Sridevi. His eyes welled. His days of fun flashed before his eyes. As he walked down the stairs towards the gate, he only thought of Rehman. He wanted to meet him, talk to him.

When he left the gate, it seemed he was born again. Everything around him looked surreal. He realized the meaning of being free. As he stood at the gate, he noticed a small wooden stool on the left side of the gate with a tatty ticket booklet. He looked around but could not find Rehman.

He crossed the road and walked to a small departmental store which was there for years.

"Salaam," Talib greeted the shopkeeper.

"Have you seen Rehman?" he asked an elderly man sitting amidst the packets of chips, chocolates, cigarettes, and other sweets.

"He used to come here every day."

"But where is he now?" Talib asked.

"After the cinema was shut down, Talib lost his means of income," the shopkeeper told him. "He tried to find other jobs but failed. He was the lone bread winner of the family, and they were pushed into utter poverty. He could not see his family suffer. He began to lose his mental state. Every day, he came here, sat on the stool, attempting to sell tickets to everyone who passed by him, knocking at the gate to let him in."

The shopkeeper told him that his family was unable to afford his treatment and had admitted him permanently to the psychiatric hospital located in the city centre, few kilometres from the cinema hall.

"One morning his room-mate found him dead. Before his death, he had been asking him to take him to Sizzlers."

Talib's eyes stung with tears. He had seen Rehman from his days of normalcy to his struggle of trying to get inside the cinema. He felt helpless.

He walked back to the gate of the cinema mall. Talib felt Rehman's presence there. He looked at the cubicle, now a bunker, where Rehman sold tickets. A security person looked through its window with a gun pointing to the road.

The stool and ticket book were lying there, untouched by Rehman for two days. Talib sat on the stool, held the ticket book close to his chest, and began to cry.

10

The Postman

Dressed in his Khaki pants and shirt, with a jute bag hanging from his shoulder, he steps out of the post office and sits on his bicycle. Ahmad is ready for his day's work.

Thirty-two-year-old Ahmad worked as a postal worker in Kashmir when there were no other means of communication except for letters and mail. He lived in the same locality where he was posted for duty. Every morning for ten years, he would get dressed and head to the post office.

The post office had stood there ever since he could remember. It was a single-storey structure, with two small rooms and one big hall. There were old wooden cupboards stuffed with papers and mail. It was barely illuminated and the smell of paper hung in the air. There were two broken benches put out for visitors, mostly the aged who often paid visits to the post office to collect letters from their children. Sometimes, aged parents could be seen discussing their loneliness and how the letters were like their lifelines.

A huge red signboard on the exterior of the building said 'India Post' in white font. There was a post box, the outside of which was rusted with the vagaries of the weather.

Ahmad would spend half an hour sifting through the mail, sometimes overhearing the conversations of lonely parents, and take his lot in his bag for delivery. To begin with, he would always ensure that he delivered the money orders sent to parents mostly by their children living outside the valley.

For hours, he would go door-to-door on his bicycle delivering letters, money orders, official documents, pictures, and parcels. He would take short tea breaks and start again. People in the whole locality, which included Hindus, Sikhs, and Muslims, knew him well. He would often sit for a brief chat with them to get updates on politics and cricket.

Whenever he delivered any good news, he would be offered sweets and given special treatment. He would often witness emotional scenes when he brought letters to parents from their children living abroad.

For years, Ahmad connected his people with those around the world. He always loved his work because he was serving his own people.

One day, as Ahmad headed for work, he was surprised to see the whole area shut down and cordoned by security forces. However, he still tried walking towards the post office. He saw barbed wires guarding the connecting lanes. There were security personnel stationed at every step. He was stopped for questioning.

"I am a postal worker. I am going to the post office," he told security personnel.

He was asked to hand over his bag. Every letter and mail were checked separately to make sure he did not carry any weapon or arms.

Ahmad himself was also frisked.

"You cannot go any further. Can't you see there is a curfew in place?"

Ahmad tried to tell the security personnel that he needed to deliver some urgent money orders.

"We have shoot at sight orders, you better get home," he was told.

Disappointed, Ahmad walked back home, after going through another round of questioning and frisking.

He later learned that a bomb blast had occurred in the main market of the valley where many were killed as well as injured. The government had imposed a curfew to maintain law and order.

Though normal life was resumed the next day, something had changed in the valley. There was more news of killings, blasts, and encounters. Scores of youths were being arrested and lodged in jails inside and outside Kashmir. There were reports of Hindus being killed by shooters (who remained unidentified) which triggered a mass exodus of the Hindu population.

Ahmad saw many of his neighbours leave. The letters for them remained with Ahmad, undelivered, as he made rounds of their locked homes.

Gradually, the mail and letters for Hindus declined and letters from prisons increased. The first letter he received was from the central jail in another city, about 300 kilometres from the valley.

As Ahmad went to deliver the letter, he came across a small green iron door which was half-open. He stepped inside. There was a small lawn that was covered with wild grass. There was a tube well in one corner which had dried up. The house was old, made of mud with wooden doors and windows. He knocked several times before an elderly lady came and opened the door.

"Salaam," Ahmad greeted her.

The woman, Amina, looked at him blankly. She was dressed in a brown *pheran*. A black headscarf covered her hair.

"I have a letter for you. It is from the central jail."

"What? Jail?" Amina smiled with joy.

She snatched the letter from Ahmad and tried to slit the envelope. Ahmed showed her how to open it so she wouldn't tear the letter.

Her eyes were full of tears as she scanned every word on the white paper. She kissed it and held it to her chest.

"I don't know how to read. But the letter has the smell of my son."

Ahmad tried to console her. He made her sit on the cemented veranda; it appeared to not have been cleaned for a while.

"I will read it to you," Ahmad said to her.

Mauji (mother), Ahmad began to read.

I know you have had sleepless nights since I left. I too have no sleep. I worry about you every minute. I have begged these people to let me go, and I have told them that I am innocent, but no one believes me.

They have lodged me in jail in Jammu. I cannot even breathe the air of my valley any more.

I get dal and roti to eat… something that I don't like. I miss the food you cooked.

Mauji, I know you are suffering because of me. But have faith in God. I will be back with you soon. There are hundreds like me who are in the jail, beaten, tortured, and some die here.

I ask you to pray for one thing for me, that I don't die here. I want to meet you before I die.

As of now, I am fine but anxious about you. Take care of your health, for my sake. One day I will be back.

I hope this letter reaches you.

Your only son,
Raja

Amina held the letter to her chest and cried.

"I want my son back. I will die without him. He is only twenty-year-old."

Ahmad asked her why Raja was in jail.

"Was he a militant or did he commit any crimes?" he asked.

"He has done nothing. His only fault is that some of his friends have taken up arms. Two weeks back, we were sleeping when they barged into the house. They took him away forcibly while I begged them to leave my son. He was never interested in anything except for his studies."

Amina told Ahmad that since her husband had died years ago, Raja would work at a local pharmacy shop as a salesperson to run the house.

"He wanted to study and give me a better life. He is the only bread-winner."

Ahmad's heart was filled with grief. As he left the house, he hoped to be back with the next letter. All his way back, Ahmad kept thinking about how Amina would survive without any income.

Nearly two weeks later, there was another letter from Raja. This time Ahmad thought of helping the woman without letting her know. He opened the envelope, put some money inside, and sealed it again.

He knocked at Amina's door. She welcomed with a smile.

"Is there a letter from Raja?" she asked.

"Yes, you open it and I will read it out to you."

"Sure, but you come inside, son, and have something to eat."

She served him tea with some biscuits. Ahmad could not say no as he did not want to hurt her sentiment.

"Now read the letter."

Mauji,

I hope you have received my previous letter. How is your health? I hope you are taking care of yourself.

I feel very scared here. Every evening I get to hear the screams of boys being beaten and tortured. I have only received a few blows till now. I dread to imagine what will happen if they do the same to me.

There are two more boys with me in the cell. They have been here for two years under the Public Safety Act. There has been no trial for them.

I anticipate and fear the same situation for myself.

I know Mauji you cannot read and write. But I am sure someone in the neighbourhood is helping you to read this letter.

I miss you every minute. And yes, I have started to pray five times a day.

I wait for the day I can see you and sleep in your lap.

Love you
Raja.

Amina was in tears but thankful to hear from her son. She too wanted to write back to him.

"Can you do me a favour," she asked Ahmad.

"Write a small letter on my behalf. It would be so kind of you."

Ahmad took out his note-pad and pen from his bag.

"Tell me what you want to say."

My beloved son,

My heart has been torn apart ever since you have gone. My life has come to a halt. Your uncle has arranged a lawyer for you. I hope you can be out soon.

This empty house haunts me. I keep talking to your photographs and hugging your clothes. I have not cleaned your room ever since you left; I have not made your bed. I want everything to be as you left it.

I spend most of my time in your room. It makes me feel your presence.

I am keeping myself alive for you, to see you one day. You are innocent and God will be with you.

I keep praying every minute for you. I pray I don't die without seeing you.

You are my heart, my life. Be strong and do not worry about me. I shall be fine.

Good to hear about your prayers.

Your Mauji.

Ahmad folded the letter and Amina kissed it. She thanked him for his support and care.

Ahmad went straight to the post office and posted the letter to the central jail.

He spent the rest of the day delivering letters and money orders.

Week after week, Ahmad would deliver letters to Amina. Routinely, he would put some money along with the letter to help Amina feed herself. She thought her son was sending the money.

Both began to develop a special relationship. Amina would wait for him and treat him to nice food whenever Ahmad came. He became a connection between Amina and Raja like he was to many others.

Sometimes, they would spend time talking about the current situation in the valley, about their past lives and families.

"You never told me about yourself," Amina asked him once as he sipped tea in her kitchen.

"I live with my old parents. My younger brother is mentally challenged which is why I had to take up a job without pursuing my studies."

Ahmad told her that he had done his bachelor's degree in science. His father had retired from work due to his heart condition. He worked in the post office for years which is how he got the job of a postal worker.

"However, now it is getting risky to do this job. There are frequent curfews and shutdowns. I face a lot of threats from security forces. I take risks because I know there are people waiting to hear from their loved ones; many await money orders to feed themselves."

"You will be rewarded for your job. My prayers are with you," Amina said to him as he got up to leave for work.

As curfews and cordons became an everyday affair, delivering letters became a difficulty for Ahmad. He would walk through barbed wires, barricades, and get into arguments with security forces, but ensure that the messages of love were delivered.

Months turned into years.

On one of his usual working days, Ahmad went to the post office to collect his mail for the day. There were letters, money orders, and a parcel. It was a square parcel wrapped in brown paper. It was addressed to one of the officials living in his locality.

Ahmad took his day's stock of delivery and left for his work. After riding on his bicycle for a few meters, he stumbled on a huge stone and his cycle lost balance. Within seconds, there was a huge blast. Ahmad was thrown off his bicycle. The letters, postcards, and money orders he wanted to deliver flew sprinkled all around him.

Injured and unable to move, he opened his eyes for a moment. He saw tattered letters landing on him. He thought of Amina, her son. He wanted to deliver the letter to her; he wanted to give her money for food. He saw a huge dark cloud before his eyes which seemed to be coming over him. He closed his eyes. Ahmad passed away.

As he lay lifeless under the pile of letters including the one from Raja, Amina sat near the door waiting to hear from her son. She waited for Ahmad to come with her letter… unaware of the incident that had occurred a few days back; unaware, that Ahmad would never come again… Ahmad – her messenger, her only connection with her son.

11

Friends Forever

Noor looked at the clock. In two hours, Soni would be back from school, and she had yet to create a perfect birthday card for her twelfth birthday. Noor has been at it for three hours. She sat on the floor, leaning against her bed. Her colour boxes, glitter pencils, erasers, and sharpeners lay scattered around her with pieces of paper. In her attempts for a perfect card, she ripped pages from her drawing copy, folded them neatly, and cut them into different shapes. She already made four of them but could not finalize any. On one card she made Soni's portrait. But as she coloured it, she felt her nose looked too big. She tried making a nice scenery on another card. On the third and fourth ones, she made flowers, but the colour scheme looked odd to her.

Now Noor, who was of the same age as Soni, was attempting to make it more personal and emotional. She wanted to catch the moment when they would sit side by side on the stairs of her house. It was hard work, but she trusted her talent in drawing and painting.

As she drew lines on the thick paper of the drawing copy, she kept her eyes on the clock. She made a beautiful picture of her and Soni, dressed in their pretty frocks, sitting on the stairs of the veranda at Noor's place. It was their favourite spot where they would sit for hours, talking and chatting. Noor took a critical look at the card. She loved it. Inside, she wrote,

My dearest friend Soni,

This day is more special to me than it is for you. It is because today, you came into this world and then into my life.

I cannot imagine any day of my life without you. You are one of the best people and friends anyone can have. I cannot be thankful enough for all the love I have gotten from you.

On this special day, I want you to know how much you mean to me. You are truly wonderful and I am so grateful to have you in my life.

I wish all the happiness and success for you.

Your bestie,
Noor

She slipped it inside an envelope that she had made from paper and decked it with stickers.

She went to her room on the first floor and sat by the window to keep an eye on the arrival of the school bus.

Soni, who belonged to a Hindu family, lived in a house just opposite to Noor's. She has been friends with her ever since Noor could remember. Their families had known each other for decades. Soni's father was a teacher in a school while her mother took tuitions at home. The two families celebrated the festivals of Diwali, Holi, and Eid together. Noor never thought there was any difference between the two families. She received the same love and care from Soni's family as she did at her own home.

The moment Soni's school bus arrived, Noor quickly put on her yellow plastic slippers, rushed downstairs, and went straight to her house. She ran to her as Soni entered the gate. Noor hugged her from the back, shouting happy birthday in her ear.

"You scared me, you fool," Soni said pushing her back.

"Come on. It's your birthday. Don't get angry," Noor told her.

The two went inside the house which smelt of freshly cooked food.

They went straight to Soni's bedroom and leaned on each other, relaxing on the bed.

"Look, what I made for you," Noor handed the card to her.

Soni looked at it in awe.

"Wow, this is so beautiful. You made it?"

"Of course, for my bestie."

"Thank you so much," Soni said as she hugged her tight.

They leaned against the back of the bed, their eyes looking at the window opposite to them. The cool autumn breeze added peace to their lives.

Soni's room was small, with walls painted light pink. There was an old two-door wardrobe that stored her clothes. The window opposite the bed had a clear view of Noor's room. There were three shelves for books on one wall. Soni loved reading, unlike Noor who had a good painter's hand. She would often tell stories to Noor while they sat in her room. Soni's mother, Anjali, would bring snacks and tea.

That evening, Noor and Soni had dinner together in the room. It was a part of the birthday celebration. Soni decided to frame the card Noor made for her.

"I will show it to my classmates tomorrow. Then, I will frame it and put it up on the wall."

It was late at night when Noor left for her home. But before going to sleep the two friends followed a ritual. They would dress in their night suits, tie their hair, and then sit on their window sills for a few minutes to say good night to each other. There were days when they spend half of the night sitting at the window and talking to each other in gestures. They pointed at the moon, the stars, and dogs that passed the lane separating their homes. They promised to be friends forever on those dark nights under the light of the moon.

It was the last night when they could enjoy each other's company.

When they woke up the next morning, the world around them had changed. The whole locality was under curfew. A huge contingent of security forces guarded their small lane. Noor sat in the living room wondering how she could meet Soni as the news of a massacre in the main city of Kashmir blared from the television. Some forty people had been killed. Her parents stayed glued to their television set with worried faces. Suddenly, sadness seemed to have taken over everything.

That night, Noor went to the window of her room as usual to meet Soni but she was not there. The lights in her room were off. At first, she thought she must have fallen asleep. But as she waited at the window with no sign of Soni, Noor grew anxious and worried. She did not understand what had happened. She wanted to call her, but she feared the security forces guarding the lane outside their homes. She waited and waited at the window for Soni to come, till she dozed off.

Noor was awakened by her mother the next morning in a panic.

"Noor, this is not the time to sleep. Get up," her mother, Henna, said to her.

"What happened, ma?"

"We are going to Soni's place. You stay here. Do not come out."

"But why are you going and why can't I come along."

"Don't ask questions. Just do as I say," Henna slammed the door behind her and locked it. She left some fruits and breakfast for her.

Noor tried to stop her but in vain.

She sat by the window. She did not understand what was happening. She saw her parents going inside Soni's house. She noticed more people joining in. There was a commotion in their lawn.

She began to worry.

Is Soni okay? she thought to herself.

She watched the commotion across the street helplessly as tears welled her eyes. She wanted to meet Soni.

Noor grew uneasy when she heard some noise coming from across the street. It turned into cries and wails. She saw Soni and her mother wailing in their lawn, their relatives trying to console them. Noor could not understand what happened but was sure something tragic had taken place.

She kept a close eye on everything that was happening in the house to ensure she did not miss any detail.

Her heart sank when she saw a body wrapped in white cloth brought out from the house. Soni and her mother followed, howling, beating their chests. The men carried the body out of the house for cremation. It did not take Noor time to understand it was Soni's father.

As she saw her best friend crying in pain, running after her father's body, Noor pulled her hair and cried like mad. Her cries remained locked in the room as she yearned to hold her best friend once.

By the time her parents were home, she had fallen asleep.

The noise from a loading truck woke up Noor the next morning. She quickly got out of the bed and looked out of the window to see what it was. Soni's uncles were loading furniture, utensils, and other household items into the truck.

Her mind was confused. She needed to know what was happening.

Without bothering to change her night suit, she rushed to her mother to find out more.

The news broke her heart.

"Soni's father is no more," Henna told her.

"But how did he die? He was okay just the last time I met him on Soni's birthday!" Noor asked, confused.

"Don't ask too many questions. They are now leaving Kashmir for another city. Today, you can meet her for the last time. But make sure you don't ask her anything about how her father died," Henna said as she tried to hide her tears.

"No, I won't let her go. I am sure if I stop her, she won't go anywhere."

With tears running down her eyes, she ran to Soni's place. The house was deserted. The furniture was all gone and it was just bare walls. She went straight to Soni's room. She was packing her books in a suitcase.

Noor ran to her and hugged her. They wept for long.

"Papa is gone, forever. He did not think once about his daughter."

Noor did not know what to say. She could not find words that could make her feel better.

"Okay listen. We must leave this place. I am leaving some books for you as my souvenir. I don't know where we are going, but I will try to write letters to you," Soni told Noor.

"I beg you not to go. I don't know why you are leaving. I cannot live without you; I can't," Noor said holding her hands tightly to stop her from going.

They hugged again, for a long time, in silence. They both knew something big had happened, and its consequences couldn't be stopped.

Noor took the books Soni gave her and left without looking back. She didn't want to show her tears to her again.

She went to her room and dumped herself on the bed and cried hard. She sat at the window, waiting to have one last glimpse of her bestie.

Noor froze as she saw Soni come out of her house with her suitcase of books. She couldn't bring herself to be by Soni's side when the moment came for her to finally leave.

Soni kept looking at Noor's room, but Noor hid behind the curtain. As Soni sat in her car, Noor screamed with helplessness and covered her ears with her hands so that she would not hear the car leaving. Before she knew it, her best friend was gone forever… to an unknown destination.

That night and all nights after that, Noor would sit by the window, looking at Soni's house. She remembered their happy days together, their window conversations. Now the house stood in front of her as a painful memory and hurtful reminder of her friend. The lights glowed there no more; there were no happy voices or sounds of laughter coming from inside; the garden was dying; dust and spider webs covered its doors and windows. With every passing day, the house began to look increasingly haunted. And every day, Noor longed to see someone come and open its doors and make it come alive again.

Every day Noor waited for a letter from Soni, but she never heard from her again.

Months turned into years…

Noor, now twenty, had passed high school and was now in college. She made many friends there, but no one could take Soni's place in her life. She would tell stories of their friendship to her classmates and college friends. Sometimes her eyes would well as she revealed the story.

One day while coming back home from college, Noor noticed dogs jumping the walls of Soni's house. Her heart ached to see how dogs began to prowl at her best friend's place.

Eight years had passed, and no one had ever come to open the gates of the house. It lay abandoned, deserted. But that day Noor decided to take care of it.

On her day off from college, she hired two labourers. She broke the lock on the main gate and stepped inside after almost a decade. Wild grass had covered the whole lawn. There were insects and rats on the lurk. She got the lawn cleaned to begin with. To enter the house, she had to break the lock again.

As she stepped inside the house, she couldn't help crying. Her days of joy with her friend were refreshed in her mind. She saw the whole house covered in dust, with mosquitoes and insects hovering all around. She dedicated a week to get the house cleaned.

She got the whole house sanitized and hired a caretaker for it. Noor paid special attention to Soni's room. She got its walls painted and the lights fixed. She even got a second-hand bed and wardrobe for it thinking that one day Soni will come back again. She could not see her room dead. She wanted to see it alive. Even though she had not heard from her for years, Noor had a strange belief that Soni would come back one day. She did not know when, but her heart knew it.

She started visiting the house regularly to see if everything was being taken care of. It gave her a strange feeling of happiness and peace.

One evening, while Noor was busy with her college assignment, there was a knock on the front door. She went to answer the knock. A young lady stood in front of her. Was it Soni? Noor had not seen her for years and did not know how she looked. Noor scanned her face carefully. She had the same eyes and complexion as Soni. But her hair was no longer black but coloured in streaks of gold. They stared at each other in surprise and silence.

"Don't you recognize me, Noor? I am Soni," the girl said.

Noor screamed with joy. They hugged and cried.

"I waited every day for your letter. You never wrote to me."

"I never forgot you for a day Noor. It is only for you that I came here, all alone."

The two felt joy as never before. The first thing Noor did was to take Soni to her home.

When Soni stepped into her abandoned house, she could not believe her eyes. The house looked as fresh as ever. She had never thought it would look this way.

She walked around the whole house, memories of her childhood coming back to her.

They went to her room and leaned on the bed. They both closed their eyes and held hands closely as they relived their childhood again.

END